This book belongs to

Aye-Aye

Richard Byrne

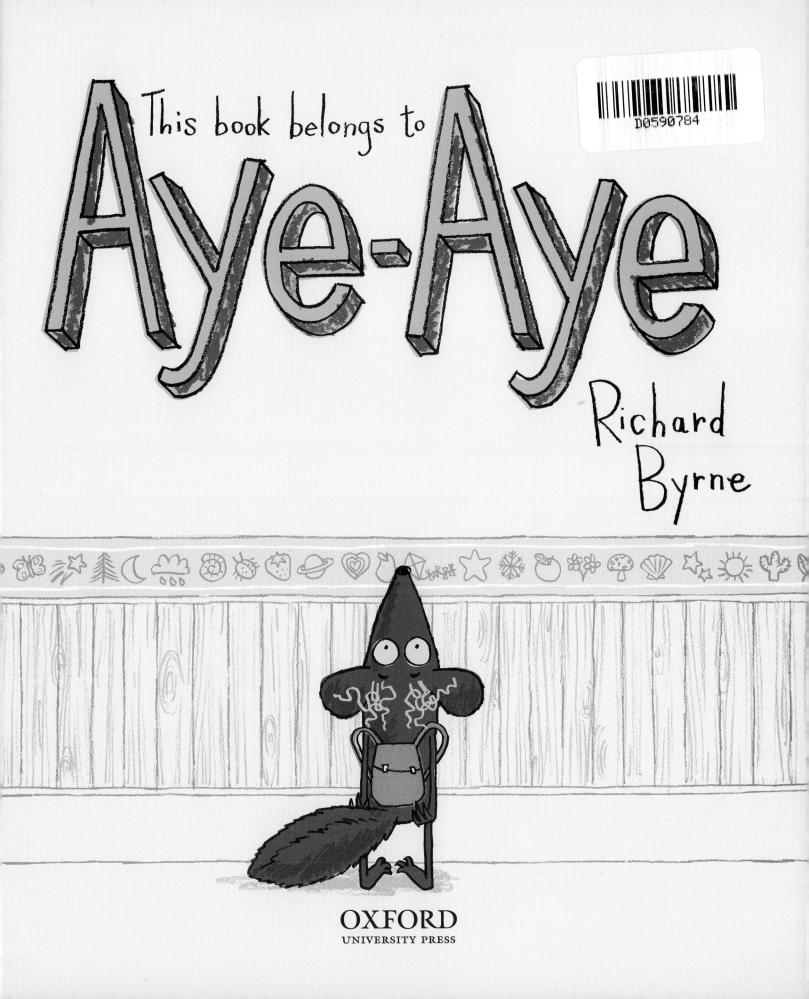

OXFORD
UNIVERSITY PRESS

Aye-Aye loved **PICTURE BOOKS**. He loved the pictures.

He loved the stories. He loved them so much that the

thing he wanted most in the whole wide world

was to be in a **PICTURE BOOK**.

Rabbit Twins

Squirrel

Duck

Aye-Aye

Frog

Mouse

My Family

My Sisters
by Duck

My brothers
by Frog

My family tree
by Squirrel

But two rabbits in Aye-Aye's new class at Miss Deer's **ACADEMY FOR ASPIRING PICTURE-BOOK ANIMALS** thought he was far too funny-looking for that.

The Rabbit Twins pointed and sniggered.
'Whoever heard of an aye-aye being in a picture book?'
they said. 'You're just not cute or fluffy enough.'

When Miss Deer told the class about a new competition,
everyone gasped. 'The most helpful animal this week,'
she said, 'will win a very special prize.'

Aye-Aye wondered if the prize
could be the thing he wanted most
in the whole wide world . . .

At home time Aye-Aye helped Squirrel to collect up the books.
They were just passing Miss Deer's chalkboard when . . .

the Rabbit Twins pushed past, singing,

'We're going to Win! We're going to Win!'

'Just ignore them,'
said Squirrel kindly.
'Tomorrow we have art
and craft,' he explained,
'so don't forget your apron.'

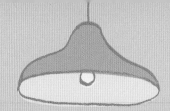

The most
creative
animal in the class
will WIN a special prize

In the morning Aye-Aye and Squirrel noticed that
the competition had *mysteriously* changed.

Miss Deer clapped her hands. 'We're going to do some painting,' she said, 'so let's put on our aprons.'

But it wasn't easy. Squirrel and Duck needed some help . . .

and by the time they were ready to paint . . .

all the paints had gone.

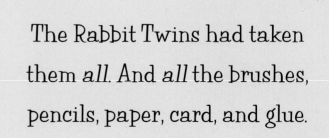

The Rabbit Twins had taken
them *all*. And *all* the brushes,
pencils, paper, card, and glue.

Aye-Aye had an idea. He picked up a newspaper and started to fold it.

The others gathered round to watch.

'Goodness! How creative!' said Miss Deer.
'And one for me, too! That's very kind, Aye-Aye.'

The Rabbit Twins looked grumpy.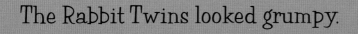

After school Frog hopped
alongside Aye-Aye. 'We've got P.E.
tomorrow,' he explained, 'so don't
forget your water bottle.'

The ~~most~~

sportiest

animal in the class

will WIN a special prize

In the morning Aye-Aye, Squirrel, and Frog noticed that
the competition had mysteriously changed *again*.

Miss Deer blew her whistle. 'We're going into the hall for P.E.,' she said, 'so let's all fill our water bottles.'

Mouse, Frog, Squirrel, and Duck needed some help . . .

and by the time they were ready . . .

the Rabbit Twins had taken *all* the balls and *all* the beanbags. The only thing left was an empty box.

Aye-Aye had an idea.
He turned the box
upside down.
Then he climbed up and
reached out his hands.
'Come on, Squirrel!' he said.

'Goodness!
What a team!'
said Miss Deer, as she
caught the first ball.

The Rabbit Twins looked
grumpier than ever.

After school Mouse scampered
alongside Aye-Aye. 'We're having
our class photograph tomorrow,'
she explained, 'so don't forget to
wear something special.'

In the morning Miss Deer took all the animals outside
for their photograph. 'Say cheese!' she said.
Everyone smiled their biggest smiles.

The Rabbit Twins looked very pleased with themselves.

'We're the cutest,' they muttered.

Later that day Aye-Aye and all his friends noticed that
the competition had mysteriously changed *again*.

The cutest,
fluffiest,
twinniest
bunnies
in the class
will WIN a special prize

And, this time, Miss Deer noticed too!

Miss Deer soon solved the mystery of how and why the words on the chalkboard had been changing all week.

'As the *naughtiest* animals,' she said to the Rabbit Twins, 'your job is to clean the classroom.'

'And this big shiny cup is for Aye-Aye because he has been the most helpful animal.'

After cleaning the classroom the Rabbit Twins decided to say sorry to Aye-Aye. 'That's a lovely prize,' said Aye-Aye's new friends.

But Aye-Aye couldn't help feeling a bit disappointed. A big shiny cup was nice but it wasn't the thing he wanted most in the whole wide world.

Then, just before home time, Miss Deer smiled knowingly
and she took a book from her table. 'It's story time,'
she said and a hush fell over the room.

'Aye-Aye loved **PICTURE BOOKS**,' began Miss Deer.

'He loved the pictures. He loved the stories.
He loved them so much that the thing he wanted most in
the whole wide world was to be in a **PICTURE BOOK**.'

And now, he was.

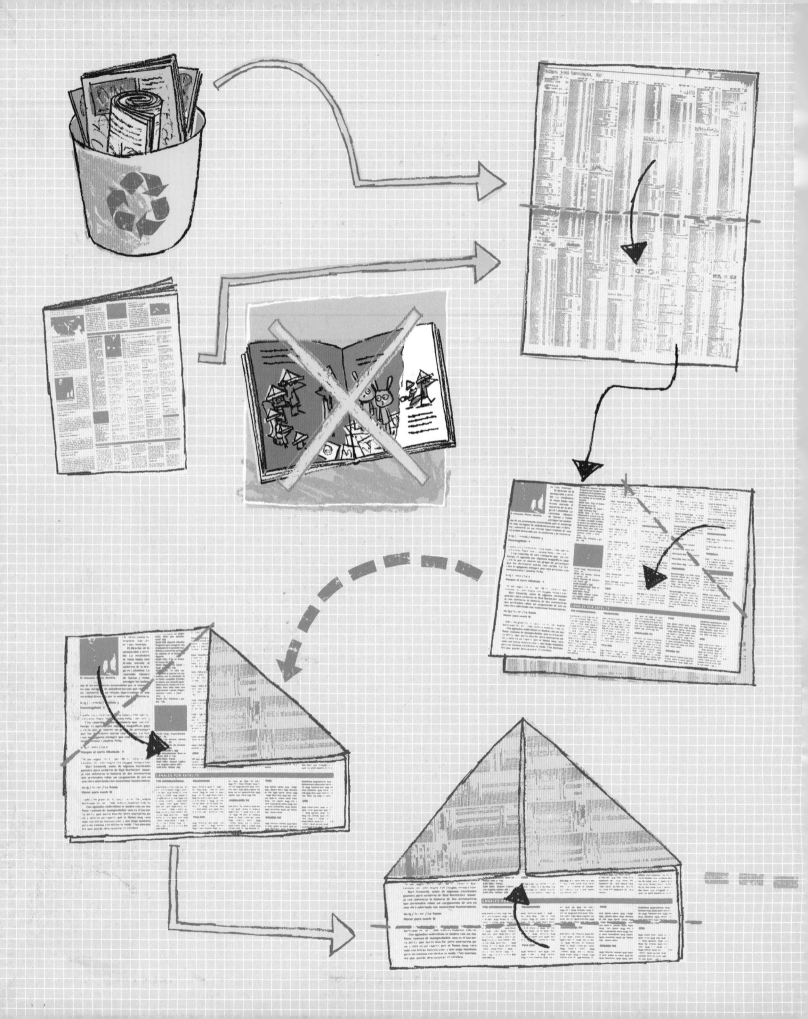